For Gay Bridgewood — it would be rude not to. J.W.

First published in Great Britain in 2006 by Andersen Press Ltd., 20 Vauxhall Bridge Road, London SW1V 2SA.
This paperback edition first published in 2006 by Andersen Press Ltd.
Published in Australia by Random House Australia Pty., Level 3, 100 Pacific Highway, North Sydney, NSW 2060.
Text copyright © Jeanne Willis, 2006. Illustrations copyright © Tony Ross, 2006.
The rights of Jeanne Willis and Tony Ross to be identified as the author and illustrator of this
work have been asserted by them in accordance with the Copyright, Designs and Patents Act, 1988.
All rights reserved. Colour separated in Switzerland by Photolitho AG, Zürich.
Printed and bound in Singapore.

10   9   8   7   6

British Library Cataloguing in Publication Data available.

ISBN 978 1 84270 571 1

This book has been printed on acid-free paper.

LON

Please renew or return Items by the date shown on your receipt

www.hertfordshire.gov.uk/libraries

Renewals and enquiries: 0300 123 4049

Textphone for hearing or 0300 123 4041
ech impaired users:

..16

The Really RUDE Rhino

Jeanne Willis and Tony Ross

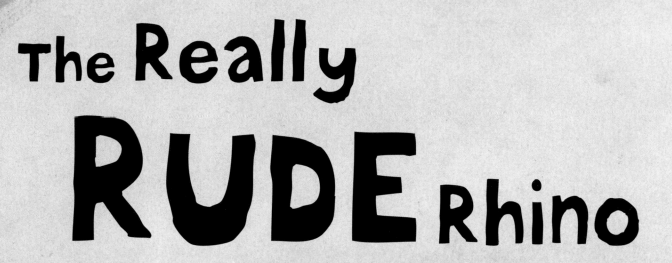

Andersen Press
London

Once upon a time, there was a Really Rude Rhino.
He was rude from the day he was born.
"What a sweet little baby!" said his auntie.

"ᴘthhhhhhhh!" went the Rhino.
"Don't be rude!" said his mother.

But the Really Rude Rhino took no notice.
He was rude to his brother.
He was rude to his sister.
He was even rude to his grandma.
"Give us a kiss," she said.

"ₚₜₕₕₕhhhhhhh!"
went the Really Rude Rhino.

"He'll grow out of it," said his granddad.
But he didn't.
The Rhino was rude from dawn to dusk.
He was rude to his friends.
He was rude to his enemies.

He was even rude to the Queen.
"How do you do?" she said.

"Pthhhhhhhh!"
went the Really Rude Rhino.
"He'll grow out of it," said the King.
But he didn't.
The Rhino was rude from breakfast to dinner.

He was rude in public.
He was rude in private.
He was really, really rude to his teacher.
"See me after school!" the teacher said.

"ₚthhhhhhhh!"
went the Really Rude Rhino.

"He'll grow out of it," said the dinner lady.
But he didn't.
The Rhino was rude from Monday to Sunday.
He was rude on holiday.
He was rude on sports day.

He was even rude on Christmas Day.
"What would you like for Christmas?" asked Santa.
"Pthhhhhhhhh!"
went the Really Rude Rhino.

He was so rude, his mother took him to the doctor.
"Open wide and say 'Ahh!'" said the doctor.

"ₚthhhhhhhhh!"

went the Really Rude Rhino.
"Will he ever grow out of it?" asked his mother.
"He's got Ruditis Rhinoceritis," said the doctor.
"There's no cure."

But there was.

Just after his fifth birthday, the Rhino woke up in a particularly rude mood and decided to go out all by himself because he was a big boy now. "Whatever you do, don't go down to the waterhole," said his mother.

"Pthhhhhhhhh!"

went the Really Rude Rhino. And off he went.

Down by the waterhole, there was a little girl eating a slice of melon very politely.

The polite little girl couldn't see the Rhino, but he could see her.
He was thinking how wonderfully rude it would be to charge out of the bushes and make her run away so he could eat the melon.
He lowered his horn. He stamped his feet and he

chaaaaaaaaaarged!

"pthhhhhhhh!"
went the little girl.

"wAAAAAAAAAGH!"
went the Rhino.

He was so shocked,
he ran all the way home . . .

and he was never rude to anyone ever again.

Other books by Jeanne Willis and Tony Ross:

9781842705261

9781842706121

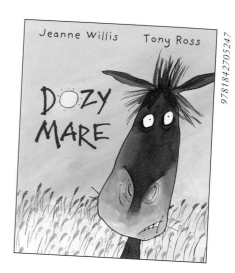

9781842705247

9781842707111

9781842705667

9781842707197

9781842704264

9781842707524